A PARRAGON BOOK
Published by Parragon Book Service Ltd, Unit 13-17 Avonbridge Trading Estate,
Atlantic Road, Avonmouth, Bristol BS11 9QD
Produced by The Templar Company plc, Pippbrook Mill,
London Road, Dorking, Surrey RH4 1JE
Printed and bound in Italy
ISBN  0-75250-897-0

# Snow White

## Illustrated by Brian Bartle

||| •PARRAGON• |||

Once upon a time there lived a 👸 called Snow White, who had skin as white as ❄ . The kind 👑 had died, and now 👧 had a wicked stepmother, who was jealous

of her beauty.

Her had a magic ,

and every day she asked it the

same question:

" , mirror on the wall,

who is the fairest one of all?"

Truthfully it always replied that she was the fairest. But 🧍 grew to be very beautiful too, and one day the 🪞 told the 👸 that 🧍 was the fairest in the land.

Her was furious and sent into the with a , telling him to kill her.

But the took pity on her, and let her run away, deep into the .

At last she came to a
 . She opened the
and went in.  There was no
one home. At a little  ,
places were laid, and  little
 were by the wall.

When the masters of the house, 7 little dwarfs, came home they were amazed to find 🧑 asleep. When she awoke, they begged her to stay, and she agreed.

Meanwhile, the 🪞 had told

her that was still alive, and dressed in disguise, the angry woman had set out to find her! She arrived at the dressed as a pedlar, and persuaded to buy some laces

for her 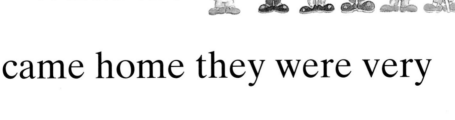. But the wicked

pulled the so tight, that

fell as if dead to the floor.

When the

came home they were very

upset, but as they untied her

, came back to life. It

was not long before the

told the , and soon she was

on her way to the once

more. This time, disguised as

a peasant, she persuaded

to take a bite of a poisoned

 . Snow White fell down

dead to the floor, and the

seven

found her there when they

returned. They cried

of tears, but they could not

wake her. They laid her in a

glass , on a

behind their .

One day a came riding

by, and fell in love as soon as

he saw her. He persuaded the

 to let

him take her  , but he

slipped and fell, jolting the

from her throat.  awoke,

and fell in love at once.

They soon married and lived

happily ever after.